AF224079

THE SHADOW I WALK IN

by Delleesa Harris

DORRANCE
PUBLISHING CO
EST. 1920
PITTSBURGH, PENNSYLVANIA 15238

The contents of this work, including, but not limited to, the accuracy of events, people, and places depicted; opinions expressed; permission to use previously published materials included; and any advice given or actions advocated are solely the responsibility of the author, who assumes all liability for said work and indemnifies the publisher against any claims stemming from publication of the work.

All Rights Reserved
Copyright © 2023 by Delleesa Harris

No part of this book may be reproduced or transmitted, downloaded, distributed, reverse engineered, or stored in or introduced into any information storage and retrieval system, in any form or by any means, including photocopying and recording, whether electronic or mechanical, now known or hereinafter invented without permission in writing from the publisher.

Dorrance Publishing Co
585 Alpha Drive
Pittsburgh, PA 15238
Visit our website at www.dorrancebookstore.com

ISBN: 978-1-6853-7390-0
eISBN: 978-1-6853-7534-8

CONTENTS

PROLOGUE

"I am afraid they will return, and next time, I will not be as lucky."

"Now Mrs. Stone, I need you to make a report and allow yourself some time for thinking. Think of anyone who has come to you with problems, anyone who has tried to hurt you, or anyone who has made threats against you. Mrs. Stone, do you have family?"

"I will need you to go to a family member's house for a few weeks while we do an investigation, I will be calling you."

"Thanks, Detective Jones."

* * *

"Hello? Hello? Anjala, are you there? This is Lonna. Hello?"

"Oh hi! Lonna, we haven't heard from you in a while. How are things going in the city for ya?"

"Not so good. I-I-I need your help. I'm in some trouble."

"Well, Lonna, that's nothing new. You're always in trouble. And you know you have burned plenty of ties back here."

"I know, Anjala. But I had no one else to call. Someone is trying to kill me."

"What? Okay, look you can come here, but if you are followed, I will kill you myself."

"Oh, thank you, Anjala. I love you."

"Yea, yea. Come on. And I want to know everything."

"Okay, but Anjala, don't tell anyone. Just let everyone think I'm on vacation, okay?"

"Yep, as long as you act like you got some sense while you're here. No trouble, please, because I'm all the way good this way, and I'm really sorry about what's going on. Oh and by the way, how long do you plan on staying?"

"A few weeks, that's all."

"Girl, it seems like you're running to me."

"Shut up. The detective told me to stay away for a while. Look, I gotta go. I will let you know when I'm on my way."

"Okay, girl. Be safe."

CHAPTER 1

Introduction

Hold on, hold on—let me go back say, my name is Lonna Stone. I'm 42 years old, and I'm from Knoxville, Tennessee, where we have very lovely people. I grew up on the eastside of Tennessee, and downtown was my favorite, especially going to the museum seeing the history artifact. And oh man, the weather is very nice!

But growing up in Tennessee was not always easy, seeing as I grew up in a large family. We had my mom, Shondra Stone; dad, Brandon Stone; sisters Monay, Tamra, and Lex; brothers June and Frank; and, well, me. Lonna. Yes, a big family. Not only that, we had about three family members staying with us. Boy, I was fed up with all the people in our four-bedroom home on Tanner Street! I mean, my cousin Lesa was rude, and her brother Rich always kept a bad odor, so no one stayed around him. Their mom, Tonya, was just yuck. They were crazy. I don't see why Mom had them there.

But anyway, I would always run to my Auntie June's house and play with Anjala; she was my favorite cousin. I was about 12 years old, and us together were like fire—everything we touched, we set on fire. We were like the Doublemint twins. We talked alike, dressed alike, even finishing each other's sentences. See, I was always the fighter, and Anjala was the lover. I took everything straight forward and didn't take shit from no one.

At the age of 15, I came across a boy named Ricky. Ricky Brown. He was about 17 at the time. I had to beat up his sister about five times, so he told me he was going to beat my ass after school. At the time, I don't believe I was ever this scared in my life. See, Ricky was on the football team, and he was very popular. All the girls loved him. Shit, no one messed with Ricky—not even me. But anyway, I told him to bring it. I was not afraid of him.

School let out about 3:00 p.m., and all I could think about was running home. As I was walking down the hall, next thing you know, I was falling on the floor. Looking behind me, it was Ricky. He had shoved me to the floor! So I jumped up and gave him a good blow to the face saying, "Yea! What you gonna do now?"

He looked at me laughing, laughing hard while saying, "You hit like a girl!"

I was confused.

He said, "Yea, you're tough, but you can't beat me."

"So, are we here to fight or talk?"

He told me, "Go home, Lonna."

"No way! You think you can just shove me around and think it's okay?"

"No, but it's best you go home, Lonna."

Days went by, and I returned to school, and Ricky said, "Hey Lonna, you hit like a girl, keep talking, and I will hit you like a man." After that, every day he said the same thing. Eventually, time passed, and Anjala told me that I should just ask him if he liked me. I was now only 16, and he was 18—I told her, "He's way too old for me! And besides, he should have never put his hands on me. I will never talk to him."

"Girl, how long ago was that? Let it go. You did beat up his sister, ya know."

Well, on my eighteenth birthday, I had a big block party.

"Look who's here, Lonna," Anjala said to me.

"Who?" I asked.

"It's Ricky Brown, and he has a box in his hand. I wonder who it's for. Maybe you, girl!"

"Nah. No way! He's not giving me," I told her.

Two minutes later, Ricky was standing in front of me, with brown sugar skin, succulent, sweet brown eyes, about 6 feet tall with the body of a hulk.

"Happy Birthday, Lonna. …Lonna. Lonna! I said happy birthday."

Shaking my head, I said, "Oh, I—Ricky, I'm sorry. My mind… Never mind. How's it going? And thank you very much."

"I wanted to give you this."

"Wait, this is for me? Why?"

"Well, because I haven't seen you in a while seeing that I'm in college now."

"Oh yea. You're right. How's that going for you?"

"It's good, but we are not here for me. We are here for you today."

"Wait. How did you know about my birthday?"

"Guss told me, and well, look, Lonna. I believe I like you. Open the box, please."

It was just jaw dropping… Boy was my jaw dropping! It was such a beautiful necklace from K.J.

"This is too much, Ricky. You shouldn't—"

"No, I should have. Because I want you to be my girl—I mean, my woman… I mean, you're all grown up now. You're a beautiful, dark chocolate woman with long hair, pretty white teeth, chunky… just my type of woman. You're strong, Lonna. Just the kind of woman I need on my side."

And that's when it all started.

CHAPTER 2

The Shadow I Walk In

So now, I was about 21—still feeling young and very vibrant. Oh wait, I am young! Silly me. Shall I continue? I'm going off course.

It had been three years, and Ricky and I were still going strong. Being with Ricky had been no walk in the park. I'd been in jail twice already because of him, doing things I'd rather not speak of… The crazy part is, I'm still madly in love with him.

Anyway, getting out this time changed me a bit after the news I was given while sitting behind bars. Three weeks pregnant. Yes, you read it right. Twenty-one and three weeks pregnant! My head was spinning, sitting, trying to understand why Ricky did not want this child. As he walked out the door, you could hear a loud bang as if he'd shattered a window; a slamming of the door. He said he had to leave; get fresh air and think about his next step, because we were not ready for a child.

Fuck what he say—I want my baby.

I discussed things with Mom and Dad, and they reassured me he would come around to it; just "be patient," they both told me.

But my sister Lex said, "Fuck Ricky. Lonna, you have us. We can help you. You don't need him. Haven't you gone through enough? You have used all of us because he wants to be a drunk, spending up all y'all's life savings, the both of you dropping out of school thinking y'all got it figured out. He's leading you down a path of destruction—you're out here robbing banks, breaking into houses 'cause you don't got shit, and he the main reason. Oh, and let's not forget your stealing from Mom and Dad. You didn't think I knew about that?"

Deep down in me, I knew Lex was right. But love hurts. Ricky was my first everything, if you understand what I mean. You have to fight for what you feel is right, and I felt that holding on to Ricky was right. There's always room for change; shit, I knew he wanted to marry me and get a big house up on Capitol Hill and put me back through school. I wanted so badly to be a crime scene investigator.

"Lex, Ricky really does love me," I tried to explain.

"No! Lonna, he doesn't. And your life ain't shit right now. And if you don't see that, then you're an even bigger fool than I thought. Look, Lonna, I'm only saying this because I love and care about you. The family loves you, and you're letting your life hang up and dry out as he pleases. You're letting way too much go."

"Okay, okay, Lex. I hear you. Thanks for the talk."

"I hope you do… Just know that I love you with all my heart, Lonna. I will always be here for you. Wrong or right, I have your back. Look, Randy is calling. I will check in with you later."

I sat in my bed wondering if I should just ask Mom and Dad for abortion money and skip town with it—go to New York and have this baby; get a good job; pay my own way through school and live life. I knew I was still young, smart, and wonderfully educated, so why not? I thought it was a great idea. I was just tired of living a lie, stealing and doing my family wrong.

"Lonna!"

What the fuck! He's always breaking my concentration.

"Lonna!"

"Yes, Ricky?"

"Did you cook dinner? I've been at work all day. I'm hungry. Shit, get the fuck up and feed me, Lonna, wit yo silly ass."

Oh God, where did I go wrong? I know he loves me, but why? Tell me why, Lord, is this the process? It was not always like this… How did this start?

"Coming, Ricky. Your food is in the oven. Let me warm it up for you. How was work today?"

"What the fuck, Lonna. You know this shit ain't easy. Every day, I wake up shaking my head not wanting to go to work. Now you pregnant, an' I got to go work all these extra hours. You need to get an abortion, Lonna. We not ready. Now come on an' feed me."

"There's a cold beer in the fridge, go and grab it while I set the table up for you."

"God dammit, Lonna. How many times do I have to tell your degenerate ass I drink Donas, not this shit, whatever it's called.

"Damn, somebody should have finished school. Maybe you could sound your words out."

"What did you just say?"

"Oh, I was just saying that's a new beer. Thought it might be good to try. They was out of stock with Donas. I will pick it up tomorrow for you. It's a special order."

Before I knew it, my head hit the table. Slap, slap, slap!—he slapped me about five times and said, "Next time, get it right. Lonna, you're so stupid. And to think you want to go back to school… For what? You're just sad, so easily controlled."

"I'm sorry, Ricky."

"Oh, and Lonna, what about this baby?"

"I was going to do it, but when I talked to Plan Parenthood and they gave me a price, I said it would have to wait. I did not have enough money for the first appointment, so…"

Slap, slap! About five more slaps came before I could even finish my words, yelling out "You bastard!" as I could only hold my face in my hand and cry.

"Look, Lonna, I'm sorry. I'm sorry I put my hands on you. This is not me. I don't understand what overcame me."

"Look, Ricky, I love you, but this has to stop. It's overbearing and exhausting. It has to stop, or I will leave you."

"Where will you go, Lonna?"

"Well, to Lex, or Mom and Dad."

"Huh? You think they want you back around?"

"No, but Lex said I—"

"Okay then, Lonna, think. Use your head. I'm all you got. Go take off your clothing. I'm ready to make love to you. I've missed you all day. I'm going to marry yo sexy ass one day.

* * *

Making love to Ricky was so passionate. He loved my curves in a way I cannot explain, never missing a beat, with a dick like a python. Despite the drinking and drugs, he kept his body in shape as if he was still on the football team; a stallion. My pussy would just drip off the thought of him laying me on my stomach, kissing me from the neck down to the tip of my toes, exploding with love juice before he could even touch the pussy, breathing hard and long. My heart began to race with every touch, every kiss; hung on every word that came out his mouth; sliding his shaft in and out of me; ever so softly grabbing my breast, and with every lick, it's as if he had to take his time with them, like each was a bowl of chocolate ice cream. Coming in seconds, treating me like a goddess…

"Oh God, I love you Ricky."

"I know you do, woman. This been my pussy since day one. Sit up and let me slide this python down ya throat."

Boy, I loved when he made me suck his manhood in and out of my mouth very slowly as he would finger me, always having the biggest orgasms…

Here I go again. I fell for it as always, I told myself as I woke up next to him. Yet another day and yo stupid ass still here…

* * *

"Oh, Anjala. He fucks me so good though."

"No! Bitch, you only think that 'cause you never had another dick in you! Take it from me, I have had plenty. Don't get stuck; they do string them along, string them along."

"That ain't true."

"Oh, yes, it is! Lonna, you only in love him 'cause you never had another man before. What about Mike from the market downtown?"

"No way. He doesn't even look at me."

"Yes, he does. I see him looking at you from time to time. It's just you who's not looking."

At this point in the conversation, Tamera entered the room.

"Hey y'all what's up? What are y'all doing?"

"Laying in the bed eating ice cream. Girl, we having our sister day."

"Well, you did not invite me. That was real rude of you."

"Sorry, Tamera. Next time, you're invited!"

"Oh, shut up, Anjala."

"Nah, Tamera. Sit down with us."

"Nah, it's okay. I just stopped by and ask about that 100 bucks Lonna owe me. Little Tim needs milk, and I'm short. Also me and June wanted to know if you was coming to Mom's birthday party?"

"Yes, we will be there, but I only have 50 bucks. Is that okay?"

"Look, Lonna, you can't keep passing me off with my money, so I guess $50 is okay. Next time, have all my money. Dad will be over later to talk to you. Oh, and learn to lock your doors around here! You not living up on Capitol Hill. One more thing, what's going on with that tummy of yours?"

"It's still here, Tamera."

"Okay. Lonna, I got to go get little Tim his milk."

"Thanks, Tamera. Tell June I said hello."

"Tell him yoself. You need to start calling and coming around more. I'm outta here."

"Okay, be safe. Tamera. Love you."

"I love ya'll too."

CHAPTER 3

About the Baby

"Anjala, I need to talk to you."

"Girl, what is it? Is he hitting you? What's wrong, Lonna?"

"No, it's not that. Well see, I found out about three weeks ago that, well, that, that I'm pregnant."

"Girl, you are playing."

"No, I'm not playing."

"Well, yeah, I know you're not. Are you happy? I mean this is so amazing. No, its astronomical! Truth is, June told me already. Why haven't you been told me about it?"

"Wasn't sure when the right time would be to tell you."

"Girl, you don't have to wait to tell me shit. You're my girl. Nah, your my sister! Don't hide shit from me."

"Well, look. Ricky doesn't want it."

"What? Hell no! What happened to my lover, lover?"

"Girl, I'm not sure. He said now is not the time for it."

"So what are you gonna do?"

"Well, it's like this. I was thinking about asking Mom and Dad for the money for an abortion, taking the money, and skipping town to New York, where I'll get a good job pay for school and live."

"Hell no! Now why would you do that, man? That's really effed-up, Lonna. Yo parents would disown you forever. Are you crazy? I mean, your mom and dad are rich on the low, but you're crazy for even thinking you can get away with that and be cool. Everyone will cut you off."

"What other options do I have, Anjala? I don't know what else to do."

"Girl, you go get a good job now and do all of what you just told me, but what about Ricky? He can't do anything. Leave his ass."

"I'm trying hard. It's really hard to do that."

"Only 'cause you're making it that way, Lonna! Look, let me set you up with Mike from the market."

"No, I can't do that. I'm pregnant."

"Girl, be just be honest with him. I'm sure he would not mind if he really likes you, but I'm telling him. I know he really likes you."

"What about—"

"Girl, don't you even ask. We will keep a low profile. Besides, you're a grown ass woman. You're about to be 22 years old! You can make your own decisions, can't you?"

"Yes."

"So stop walking that man's shadow and walk on your own."

"Okay, girl. Set things up with Mike."

"Will do, Lonna. But you know, I remember when you were scared of no one, givin' Ricky that blow to the face when you were about 15 or so. That's what made him want you, because you were strong, Lonna, and you still are. Get your balls back and move forward."

"Okay, okay, you made me feel a lot better. I needed those words of encouragement."

"Oh, and I know this job you can get; it's paying like $18 an hour. I can't go because I have smoked too much weed, but they are having open interviews tomorrow. I gotta wait till my system clears because I would like to work their, too."

"Where is it located?"

"It's on Capitol Hill."

"That's my dream to even walk the streets of Capitol Hill!"

"Well you would have been there if you would not have spent all your scholarship money up."

"Don't do that. Anjala. I already feel bad."

"I'm just saying, your mom and dad worked real hard for that money for all of you, and mostly you because they saw potential in you. And let's not forget who else helped—Monay and Frank helped them help you," Anjala continued. "Your siblings are spoiled, and even they managed to finish school, get good jobs, and are working upwards to Capitol Hill as we speak, and you know your sister was broke—she wanted her money back. Even more reasons for you to get your life in order, be a high roller with them, and pay everyone back. Oh, and how far along are you?"

"About three months, I believe."

"Yes! Girl, what you think you gonna have?"

"A boy."

"Dad, where did you come from?"

"Your door was open. How's my baby girl?"

"I'm a good, Dad. How long have you been standing there?"

"Long enough. Anyway, I came to give you some money. I know the diner is not giving you much to live off of, and we will leave the rest where it lies."

"Thanks, Dad. I love you."

"I know, princess. I know."

"Dad, you're the best. I promise to pay you back—"

"Don't worry about that. What you do for me is go back to school. Me and Mom only want what's best for you, and we expect it to be done soon. Don't tell her I gave you this. And no more lies, Lonna. I'm tired of them and will no longer deal with it."

"Yes, Dad, I hear you."

At that point, Dad switched his attention to Anjala.

"Hello Anjala, how's your mom?"

"She's still cooking for the White House, always in D.C."

"Good. Tell her I said hello and to let me and Shonda know when she's back. Shonda would like to cook for her."

"Haha, okay Uncle B! Okay, Lonna, I gotta go to work."

"Wait, I thought you were off."

"I picked up a shift."

"Heffa, when were you going to tell me?"

"I was, we just got caught up."

"Haha, okay. Have a good night—and don't take no one home!"

"Hmmm, I will think about it."

CHAPTER 4

Anjala

Working at the Foxes was getting on my last nerve. I could never find a real man with this type of job. Shit, I'm ready to settle down, have a life, be a wife and mother to some snot-nosed kids…

I wondered what Lonna was doing.

The music was playing really loudly in the background for some reason today. Maybe this was not for me anymore. Then I could hear Mack: "Here's the wonderful Ms. Lucky Number One, who you all been waiting for! Spice!" That was my cue.

So I gulped down my drink and headed to the stage, praying this would be my last day here. Seeing about 30 men, I began to twirl around the pole, doing my thang, feeling the few drinks I had dropping down and spreading my legs, waiting for that hot $50 to hit my pantie line, or one of these ballers to ask me to go home with them, so I could make a quick $200 for the night.

As I opened my eyes, I saw Mike from the downtown market.

Oh, shit—no! He can't see me like this… Damn!

I hurried up in the spotlight, cleaned up, and hit the floor to talk to Mike.

"Hey, hey Mike, hey. How are you doing? You're the last person I expected to see in a place like this! It doesn't seem like your style."

"No, no. It's not, but I'm here with a friend for his bachelor party."

"Haha, this is why I picked up today! Must have been meant to run into you. It's for Montez, right?"

"Yes."

"He's a regular, and he told me he was going to marry his dream girl. Let him know I'm happy for him, will you?"

"Sure will. Anyway, is this what you do on a regular basis for work?"

"Yes."

"How long?"

"Three years now."

"Oh, okay."

"Yeah, well. You know…it pays the bills at the end of the day, and beats depending on my mom, ya know?"

"I guess that's cool."

"Well, look, I wanted to hook you up with my sister Lonna, the one you're always cutting your eyes at when we are in the market?"

"Yeah, she is beautiful, man. Wait, does she work here with you?"

"No. She works at the diner over on Harris Street. You know, Kim's Family Diner?"

"Oh, yes. I've been there a few times."

"Well, look, she's in a situation, and I was kinda hoping you can be her backbone, ya know?"

"What do you mean? Anjala, I'm not understanding what you're saying."

"Well, she's with this guy, and I'm trying to get her to see she has options. He's no good for her, so I was hoping to set you up on a blind date."

"Look, Anjala, I don't need a woman with problems. I need a woman who is free with a brain and doesn't have to sneak around until she is ready to leave a man. See, I'm straightforward and a damn good man. That's why I'm single. The bullshit is for the birds. You understand. Anjala, I have goals in life and would like to accomplish them, owning a few markets of my own, having kids and a wife who don't want for anything but my love, ya dig? Holla at me when she is free and ready for a real man."

"No, look, all I'm asking is you give it a try. Be the reason why she leaves him. She has never been with another man; that is why she is so trapped."

"Okay, look, just a try, because I like her and I trust you and know you really well, Anjala, so I feel you would not lie to me. Look, I need to go and enjoy my time and back my friend up, okay? Here's my number, so we can set things up." He gave me his number.

Damn, I wished I would have turned up on his ass and put the cat in the bag. He was like chocolate thunder walking around. Short with a medium-built body, always looking like he worked out, and I always felt he was very polished; but seeing him outside of the market today told it all. Everything he had on matched to the T! Wow, I'm getting wet just thinking about it!

Oh, and must I say, he has cat eyes and very clean, white teeth, nails clean, and smelled like you could just gobble him up with one bite…

"Anjala, Anjala? Did you hear me?"

"Oh, yes, I heard you. I'm sorry—it's just the music and my thoughts."

"Nah, you good. Like I said I'm 'bout to go catch up. You be cool. We will talk soon."

"Okay, goodnight, Mike."

When the nights get cold and you wish you had someone to warm you up, just pull your blanket and pillow close. That should do the job…

Oh no that sucks. Very shitty.

"Anjala, get your ass on stage."

"Damn it! Better be some money on that stage, Tonney! I got bills to pay, and you are not about to be taking all my money; not tonight sucka."

"Man, get yo ass on that stage and do what you do best, Anjala. FYI, guys that's in here tonight is a money crowd. They here for a bachelor party, so bring yo A-game."

"Tell me something I don't know."

"Oh, you also have private shows."

"Wait, can Kasidie do it? I'm not ready."

"You have to do it. It's a special request."

"Damn, damn, damn, Tonney! What the eff—? Okay."

* * *

I looked down at the man grabbing on my leg. I had never seen this man before. He was a tall redbone with grey eyes, very tall with a slim build and clean nails, and I love a man with clean hands. Smelling like a million bucks, you could tell he paid a pretty penny for it.

"Hey lady, what's your name?"

"Spice."

"Spice, huh?"

"Yeah, that's my name."

"Well, Spice, I'm Eric."

"Hello Eric, what do you want from me? I'm trying to dance."

"I was told you're the best here, so I figured I would ask for you and see what you're about."

"I'm already doing a private dance. How did you get back here anyway?"

"Money talk; bullshit walk. You know what they say. Look, mama, I'm new here. I will give you $500 for a night if you come home with me."

Well, damn. Why so much? Angel said $500… You got bills to pay. You better take him up on that.

"Hello, did you hear me? Five hundred for the night."

"Okay, look. Let me finish my private dance first."

"Okay, yeah, I'm here with them anyway. Do yo thang, baby girl."

* * *

"So where are you from, Eric?"

"Cleveland."

"Cleveland? Okay, I heard some okay things about Cleveland. What brought you here to Tennessee?"

"I wanted change. My wife died two years ago due to cancer, and well, I wanted to start over fresh; see new things; get away from the house we brought together. Try and fade some things of the past, ya know? What about you, Ms. Spice?"

"It's Anjala."

"Okay, Anjala. Tell me about you."

"I've been here all my life. My mom's a cook for the White House and rather than depending on her, I chose to live my life how I want to. I'm 24 years old, and I have no kids of my own, so I guess I'm living. By the way, how old are you?"

"I'm 35. Why did you choose to be a stripper?"

"Well, 'cause it was quick and easy money, and I have the body for it. Just got caught up with it. Wait, is this Capitol Hill?"

"Yeah, why? Because I have never been in this part of the city. Only the rich live here."

"Nah, you don't have to be rich; just stable. Shit, I bet with all the money you make every night, you can pull yourself up this way."

"Not a chance."

"Don't ever say never until you try, Anjala."

Hmm…he might be the one. Shit, he's going up on Capitol Hill—he got money, an' the way he's talking, he knows what he's doing!

Looking at all the beautiful lights, I felt as if I was dreaming.

"You hear me, Anjala? This is the place."

"Wow! This is nice. Is this your condo?"

"Yes."

"What do you do for a living?"

"I'm an accountant."

"Really? Wow, okay."

"Hahaha, you're funny, Anjala."

"Look, why me out of all the girls in the club and $500 for a night?"

"Because I was told about you, but when I spotted you, I spotted you and only you. When I saw you, I was like: She looks likes she's from an Indian tribe—long, silky black hair hanging all the way to your ass, not a piece of fat hanging on your body, looking like a hot cup of coffee on a cool morning. Very definitely sparkling like gold in my eyes, and I thought, she's mine, and if for only one night, that's fine with me. So we are here now, Anjala. What would you like to do?"

"How about a drink and some Marven Gey?"

"Oh yeah, you're talking my language now. What kind of drink do you want?"

"I will take a dark n' stormy."

"What's that?"

"Something that's gonna put you on yo ass, haha. Just something I made up for myself. So Eric, do you have kids?"

"Yes, two girls."

"How old are they, if you don't mind me asking?"

"I don't talk about my girls to no one, and we are not at that level, yet so maybe if you decide to be my right hand and have my heart, we will go into more details about them."

"Okay, I can understand that."

"Let me tell you this, Anjala, if you want to be my woman, you have to polish up and get out that stripping shit. A woman like you doesn't need to be in a place like that and hooking up with bad guys that you don't even know. Not knowing the good from the bad and the real ugly. You're sitting on my couch because I said I would give you $500 for a night. How safe is that?"

"Look, is that what you got me here for? 'Cause you can open the door, and I can walk out just as I walked in."

"Nah, baby girl. Once you in, you in, but I'm just trying to school you on some things. Now I'm gonna give you the $500 because I am a man of my words. Do you really think I would bring you to a place like this and do you dirty? I would have just taken you to a cheap motel downtown; a hole in the wall joint. So the money is on the table, but you're gonna have to show me what you're gonna do for it."

"Really?"

"Yes."

"Well, change the music, and let me show you why I'm so good at what I do."

"Okay, baby girl. Do yo thang."

* * *

"Anjala, it's 9:00 a.m. Let me take you home."

"Wow, already?"

"Yeah, come on."

"I don't even remember falling asleep…"

"Same here. I do know one thing though—you let Spice out on me. Everything about you was good, and I mean everything."

"Wait, did we use protection?"

"Sure did. See, that's why I said you need to polish up. Hang around me, and I will have you so polished, your family will not recognize you. Let's go eat first then I will take you home."

Chapter 5

Girl Talk

"Hey girl, where have you been all night I was up waiting for your call? I also called you, and your phone kept going to voicemail."

"Oh gosh, Lonna, I got the giggles, and I'm in a good mood."

"Girl, what is going on? What happened to you calling me to get to the point?"

"Okay, okay. I met this guy name Eric last night. He offered me $500 for a night, so I agreed, and honey, let me tell you, it was the best night of my life! I mean, he's so polished, so gentle just all in one. He say he's an accountant, but a man of his stature don't rub me like an accountant; more like a thug maybe. I'm not sure but."

"Now, why would he give you that type of money for one day, ask yourself that."

"Because, girl, he is smooth."

"Anjala, what I tell you about trusting these niggas like that?"

"Like you got room to talk. By the way, I ran into Mike from the market."

"Did you?"

"Yep. He said he is willing to hook up with you."

"No way!"

"Yes way, bitch. I told you I got you, boo."

"I don't know about this…"

"Stop it. We will work on this together."

"Let's change the subject. And you still not off the hook for the stunt you pulled last night. You know it's Mom's birthday today, so we gotta get moving."

"Yeah, I know. I got her something really nice and a lil' something for you."

"What is it? What is it? Show me!"

"Okay, but don't cry. Lonna, come outside."

"Oh my God, Anjala, you didn't!"

"I did, girl, I did because I love you that much! Plus you 'bout to have a baby. You need to get around."

"Girl, how fast does it go, 180 miles?"

"Nope, 270. This is a Hennessey Venom."

"How did you pay for this? This is insane."

"Noneya, haha! Here's the keys. Enjoy your ride. You're moving up in this world. Capitol Hill Lonna is on her way!"

"Okay, girl. I'm about to go get ready. I will see you at 6:00 sharp."

"Okay, Anjala. Thank you so much! I love you."

I was looking in the mirror, telling myself I needed to work on things, and here this ass went yelling my name: "Lonna, Lonna, who's car is this in the driveway?"

"Oh, hi honey. It's mine."

"And how did you afford that?"

"I didn't."

"Let me guess, your fucking parents brought it for you, trying to show me up yet again."

"No, Anjala got it for me."

"What! You fucking or something?"

"No, that's my sister."

"Look, Lonna, I'm trying my best to provide for you, and you're still giving them sob stories."

"No, I'm not. I haven't told anyone anything. I'm trying to deal with you, Ricky, and you're making it hard for me to do that. Always telling me I'm stupid or slapping me in my face, talking about my family. What about all the shit I've done for you? I'm lucky—you're lucky—my family even deals with you. I thought you loved me, or was that just a figment of my imagination or a wet dream, huh? You fucking tell me, Mr. Ricky Brown."

"Look, Lonna, I'm sorry!"

"The hell you are!"

"Lonna, will you be Mrs. Brown? And you can keep the baby. I mean, I promise I'm trying to change. I would love to be the one you gave your heart to again."

"I don't know, Ricky. There's a lot we have to work on before I say yes."

"What?"

…and before I could say another word, he slapped and punched me.

"See! This is what I'm talking about. But you feel as if you're changing or gonna change."

Next thing you know, I'm in the air and on the floor with him looking down at me, saying, "I will be damned if you leave me and damn if you don't marry me, hoe. Think about that."

"If my family knew you put your hands on me, they would…"

"What? Bitch, I'm not scared of your weak-ass family."

"Look, Ricky, my mom's party is in two hours. I have to go."

"Yeah, well, yo ass better be home before dinner get cold. And to think I just bought yo ass a Auriya 18k two-tone engagement ring for $504,780.74 to prove my love for you. You're worthless, Lonna. You and that baby need to just die."

On the drive to Mom's, all of what he said to me would not stop replaying in my head. I kept telling myself I needed to get out, and I needed to check on this baby. As much as he's been hitting me, who's to say the baby was not already dead.

* * *

"Hey Lonna we all have been wondering when you would get here."

"Yes, family, I'm here. Hello Mama, happy birthday! How old are you now, 18?"

"Oh, girl, you always know how to make me smile. Give me a hug and a kiss. I miss you."

"I miss you, too, Mom. It's only right you and Dad…"

"Hush, girl. Save it for another day, because today is mine."

"Hey Lonna, how are you? Long time no see."

"What's up Frank, what are you up to these days?"

"Shit, you know me, hitting my job up on hours. I just became partners with the company, so I own 70 percent of it now, but I still work like I'm getting paid hourly. How about you, pretty lady?"

"Umm, well, I'm still working at the diner, and I'm about four months pregnant now."

"Oh yeah, I forgot, sis, congrats. What are you hoping for?"

"It doesn't matter to me."

"That's good, sis. I'm extremely happy for you and can't wait to see him/her. Sis, let me ask a real question, and I need you to be straight with me. Is Ricky hitting you or treating you bad?"

"No, why do you ask that?"

"Because Mom and Dad are concerned about you, saying they will not step in until you say you're ready for it to be over, and I see your face, so don't think no one has noticed it. But you know I don't care what Mom and Dad are saying. I might be one educated man, but I know goons, shooters, rostas, killers…you name it. I can get it covered. They will body and toe tag him in a heartbeat."

"No, Frank, everything is good. I promise."

"Okay, don't think I can't tell you were crying. And just to let you know, no matter the amount of makeup you put on, it will not cover the swollen cheek you have. I'm a smart man, sis. You like it, but I sure as hell don't love it. Let me know when you're ready, or I will take action without your approval."

CHAPTER 6

Mom's Party

"Hey Monay, who cooked this food?"

"Girl, you know I did. Where have you been?"

"Wait, I should be asking you the same thing. And I've been around. How's life with James?"

"It's great, though I have not told Mom and Dad that we are having twins."

"What! Oh my gosh, that's great! Wait—oh gosh, that's a lot! Boy, girl…what you having?"

"We don't know yet, but I hope it's girls."

"Aww, sis, I'm happy for ya'll."

"Thanks, Lonna. I also heard that you are expecting a little bundle of joy, too."

"Oh, yes, I am."

"So what are you expecting, boy, girl?"

"Well, I don't know yet, but it doesn't matter either way. I'm fine just knowing I have a lil' one to look after. Monay, are you working? Because having twins is hard work. You're talking double everything."

"No, I'm not working, but James has it under control. You know I haven't worked in years. Once he got his degree in psychology,

I've been at home. He makes good money, and can you believe he's on his way to be a neurosurgeon? It will keep him away from home a lot…just the way I like it, hahahaha! It keeps us missing one another, and the spark stays alive a lot longer. You always need space with your spouse, no matter how much you feel your love can never be broken."

"Yeah, I guess you're right, sis."

"Call me more often. I understand life will gobble you up, but still stay in touch, sis."

"I love you."

"Love you, too, Lonna. Now let's go party."

* * *

"Well, everyone, if we all can bring our cups and gather around the table, Shondra and I would like to raise a toast. As we all know, we are family. Family is to stick together in times of need and in times of love. Shondra would like for you all to know she's very pleased with the extravagant gifts that were bought for her as always."

"Yes," Mom added. "It is always an elegant surprise to have you all over; so many beautiful faces and so much love to give. Thank you all. Again raise, your drinks, ladies and gents, and drink. Now, it's time for you all to go home. No late nights here. Love you all!"

"Okay, Mom," I told her. "I'm on my way to the diner. See you tomorrow."

* * *

"Hey Dex, how are you?"

"I'm good, Lonna. By the way, how did you get here so fast? Ya husband buy you a new wip?"

"No, but yes. The new car is from Anjala."

"Umm, you sure you need to be working here? Between your husband and family, you're pretty spoiled rotten."

"No, Dex, I'm not. I just have people who care about me, that's all."

"Okay, Lonna, whatever you say. Now get to work. There're a few gentlemen down at the end from out of town, so make sure all their food is made to their liking and be really nice. We don't know how long they will be here, so we want good reviews. See to it that they are very happy."

"Right. Like you have to tell me that, but okay, Dex."

* * *

"Hello and good morning, gentlemen, my name is Lonna, and I will be your waitress. Now, how may I help y'all?"

"Hello Lonna, we all would like to have your breakfast special: eggs over easy and one extra sausage on each plate, with chives and cheese on our eggs."

"Would you like coffee with that or fresh orange juice?"

"We will start with coffee and then have orange juice when our meals are ready."

"Okay, anything else I can do for you while you wait?"

"Yeah, you can put on some relaxing music?"

"Okay, will that be all?"

And then, right there, you know how you always have that one guy who has to open his big-ass mouth?

"No, that's not all. How about you give me your number? Will you be the one doing all the cooking as well? I'm sure you can put your foot in it."

"I'm sorry, sir. I did not catch your name."

"Bill."

"Well, Bill. I can't do that. I am a married woman."

"I don't see a ring on your finger."

"It's in the shop, hun. Let me go get your food ready."

While the out-of-towners, who I came to learn were named Eric, Bill, and Jordan, were sitting eating, I could over hear Eric saying, "These people down here cool as fuck, but don't let them fool you. Stay focused. We are here on a two-year business trip only. We need to see how shit goes an' make our moves accordingly."

Bill said, "I'm telling you, we need some bitches who gonna help us move through the city on some quick shit, and a stash house."

"I got one already," Eric said. "Her name is Anjala, a stripper who works at that one spot we were at The Foxes. She seems real solid though, so that's one down."

Oh, shit, Anjala! He is talking about Anjala! I should tell her? Nope, let her find out on her own… She needs to know to stop trusting every man she climbs in bed with. As soon as I was trying to get a lil' closer to hear more, the bell on the door went off. Damn, a customer is here…

I turned around to say hello and was caught off guard. It was Mike, Mike from the market.

"Well hello, Lonna. That's your name right?"

"Umm, yes. How did you know that, if I may ask?"

"I ran into your sister over at The Foxes."

"Hmm, you don't seem like that type of guy."

"I'm not. I was just there for a bachelor party. Any way, she told me you were interested…"

"Wait, I never said that. She told me you were always cutting your eyes at me in the market."

"True, I do. So maybe I'm the one who's interested, but she did tell me you're having man problems."

"Well, she has a big mouth, and that was not her place to tell you that."

"Chill, lil' lady, it's best I know sooner than later, so let me be the judge of wanting to continue my gaze on you."

"Okay, you're right. So Mike, how old are you?"

"Twenty-six. And you, Ms. Lonna?"

"I'm 22."

"And you have man problems? Look, I'm gonna cut this conversion short. I know you need to get back to work. Here's my number."

"You should be as free as a bird right now."

"Well, you call me if you have a change of heart, and maybe we can have dinner, a movie and talk more. You seem a lot older than 22… Let's see where things can go."

"Okay, thank you, Mike."

"Hey, hey Lonna, what's up with the orange juice, woman?"

Ugh. They are rude…

"Hold on, guys. I'm going to get it now."

"Hey Lonna, I thought you said you were married, shorty."

"I am."

"Then why you over there talking to that guy blushing, shorty? You really should let me be that one who can make you show that pretty smile all the time and get you out this fucked up ass job you got. How much you make, like 200 a week?"

He got to be kidding me, but he is cute looking like the game…

"I'm sorry, Bill, but that is not be necessary, nor is it your problem. I'm good."

"Okay, shorty. I'm just saying, I can give you that life of freedom. You just need to be that down ass bitch I for me, know what I'm saying?"

"No, I don't. And I am not a bitch, thank you."

"Nah, shorty. I'm just saying a good woman, that's what I meant."

"No, thank you, Bill. That was nice of you to offer."

"Anytime, shorty. I will be around if you change that thought, make you mine and turn you into that elegant woman I see in you—nothing but elegance 24/7."

"Bill, enough."

"Okay, shorty. Sorry."

"Okay, Lonna. That's all we need. Come back after we leave," the Eric guy told me.

* * *

"Hey, Dex. It's hot as hells balls in here. What's up with the air conditioning?"

"Oh, someone stole it… I didn't tell you that?"

"Nope, you did not tell me that. How long?"

"About a month ago."

"Damn, Dex."

"Well now you know. Now, get back to work. We have people all over today, Lonna. Hurry up."

"I just love you, Dex."

"And you know I love you, too, Lonna. Now go make money, honey."

* * *

"Look, like I said, we push this dope through the city. The mark is Capitol Hill. All these rich folks stay up there, and we need their money. They don't have shit else to do with it. Jordan and Bill, get on ya shit and find some women. Maybe a white woman who can move us through Capitol Hill."

"Now, E, you know snowflakes are off the market."

"Man, this is about money. I don't care if you got to slay her—get it done."

"We got you, E. So where we gonna tell people where we are from?"

"Florida. Look, leave Lonna a nice tip. I'm bout to go meet up with Anjala. Shit bout to take off. Bye Lonna! Have a good day, lady! See you another day!"

"Okay, thank you, have a good day."

Yep, and the boys got you…

"Yo, Lonna, come over here."

"Yes, Bill?"

"Well, we 'bout to pull out, and I wanted to leave you a good tip, ya know, show our hospitality. We haven't had service like this since we been here."

"That's fine, Bill."

"Look, here's $300."

"Wait, why am I so lucky for a $300 tip from you?"

"'Cause I like you, an' I want you to know money is not a problem for me."

"That's nice, Bill, and the compliment was great, but I can't take this."

"You have no choice, because I left it on the table, and now I'm walking away."

"Wait, Bill, what is it that you do for an occupation?"

"I'm a pharmaceutical, shorty. That's big money, ya dig?"

"Man, let's go. Leave the woman alone, Bill, we got shit to do."

"A'ight, chill, Jordan. In a minute, son."

"You don't talk like you pass out meds, Mr. Bill."

"Well, don't let the talk fool ya, shorty. A man can do and be anything. The words that come out a man's mouth don't matter about their occupation. Be cool, take that money, and go get a nice dress, so when I see you again, I can tell you how gorgeous you are."

"Okay, Bill. See you later."

"Lonna, you got customers. Come on now."

"Okay, Dex, I got you."

Then my phone began to ring, and who else could it be but Ricky? I did not want to answer, so I nonchalantly picked up: "Yes Ricky?"

"Lonna, where are you?"

"You know I'm working. What is it?"

"Lonna, I'm hungry. Come home and feed me."

"Are you serious?"

"Look, baby, I'm just playing. Let me take you out tomorrow after your night shift is over. I have a surprise for you baby."

"Okay, Ricky. That sounds great. How should I dress for this surprise?"

"Put on your best 'cause this 'bout to be one hell of a night."

"Okay, bae. See you soon."

"Oh, and Lonna?"

"Yes?"

"You know I love the fuck out of you? I'm trying to fix our problems. Just give me time."

Chapter 7

"Dang, I'm tired."

Anjala had been at work all night dealing with crazy men walking in and out the dinner, and she replied, "Girl, tell me about it. Shit. Eric came over again."

"Girl, what does he do?"

"He told me he's a banker. I finally got a good one. He says he is going to polish me up, and I can leave the club soon."

"Just be careful, Anjala. You don't know him. Don't be trusting everything that comes out his mouth."

"Look who's talking, girl, bye."

"Oh. Did you send Mike to the diner? How did he know I worked there? Let me guess, you told him."

"Yes, Lonna. I did, because you need change. Now, let's go to this appointment."

* * *

"Lonna? Lonna Stone, the doctor will see you now."

"Hello, Ms. Stone."

"Hello Dr. Sims, how are you?"

"I'm good, Ms. Stone. So you are having a lot of morning sickness, I see, that is a phase most women experience. It should go away soon. In the meantime, I can give you this candy. It should help settle your morning sickness. You are also due for an ultrasound today, and we might be able to see the sex of the baby and get the correct due date of the baby, though that does not always mean your baby will come that exact day. You may have to be induced, or he/she may come early or past your due date. Are you taking your prenatal pills? It's been a while since I have seen you. Make sure you stay on top of that. Also, have you had any pain or discomfort?"

"No, none."

"Good, you can't even tell there's a baby in there. Now, let's get started. Are you ready?"

"I know it's a boy, Lonna."

"Shut up, Anjala, you don't know. I can't wait. Ricky wants to take me out tonight, so I can surprise him with the sex of the baby."

"Girl, you sure you want to go out with him?"

"Yes, Anjala, I do. He's trying."

"Yeah, sure he is. You should really talk to—"

"Are you ready, Ms. Stone?"

"Yes."

"It's a boy, Ms. Stone! Congratulations! Are you happy?"

"Yes, I am. It's the best thing I have heard all day."

"Okay, go out and tell Mrs. Patty you want a two-week follow up and put your due date on a calendar. Tell your mother I said hello."

"Thanks, Dr. Sims."

"Okay, Ms. Stone, see you soon."

* * *

"Okay, sis, I'm gone. I'm about to hook up with Eric and fuck his brains out."

"Yuck, okay, girl. Bye."

I called Mom first, as always, to let her know the good news.

"Hello Mama! I have great news for you and Dad."

"What is it, Lonna?"

"Well, we are having a boy!"

"Oh, Lonna, that's great. I'm really happy for you! What's his name going to be?"

"I don't know, Mama. Me and Ricky will have to talk about it."

"Okay, baby girl. Well, you do that and get back to us."

"Wait, Mama, I have your money."

"No, you keep it. I'm glad things are looking up for you. Just remember what I told you."

"Yes, Mama, I will."

"Oh, and Lonna, are things okay with you and Ricky?"

"Yes, Mama, we have our problems just like you and Dad, but we are working on it. And things are getting better. Look, Mama, this is him. I will call you later … Hi Ricky, I'm on my way to the dress shop, and then I will be on my way to cook for you."

"Okay, baby, see you soon."

* * *

"Hello, my name is Donna, and I am here to help you. Please be sure to let me know if you may need me."

"Okay, Donna, I'm looking for a very extravagant dress. This is a very special night for me."

"Hmm, someone is a lucky lady. He's probably going to propose to you."

"Yea, I'm sure he is."

"How about this red dress here? This is a ballroom gown with five one-karat diamonds around the neck. Asking price is $8,000, but if you sign up for a credit card with us today, you walk out with the dress with no cash down and get a 50 percent discount. Also payments can be made monthly."

"Oh, really? Let's do it. That sounds great. I get to keep some money in my pocket today."

"Let's try it on."

My thoughts were going 90 miles per hour. Things were going good for me. Shit, Ricky was becoming much better on how he talked to me, hadn't been hitting me, and was making love to me like no other—and I mean real love. My stomach was beginning to grow. Hell, he had a surprise for me, and I had one for him. I wondered what he was going to think about us having a boy. And let's not forget about the job Anjala told me about up on Capitol Hill. I had an interview with them on Thursday. Yes, they finally called me back. I was so happy, just so happy. I had to write a poem:

Poem of the Day
When the road to recovery gets dark
Along the way, and you can no longer
See, just keep telling yourself it's not as
Dark as it may seem. Just look to the sky
And ask the Lord, please, oh Lord, guide me so
I may see.

"Lonna, Lonna, you ready, babe?"

"Yes, Ricky, I am in the room."

"Well, come on. We don't want to be late… Damn, girl! You look amazing! I mean, shit do you belong to me? I want to fuck you right now. Just lift that dress up and slide them panties half way down, lift that leg over the bed show me those hills, and let me slide this big dick in that warm pussy."

"Oh, gosh, Ricky. Stop it! Let's go before we are late! But if you are a good man for our date night, I just might let you fuck me like that in the truck."

"Damn, girl, now you talking my language."

* * *

"Reservations for two."

"Yes, and your name?"

"Brown."

"Oh, Mr. Brown, right this way… Table for two, please, have a seat, your menus are on the table, and Jesica, your waitress, will be with you soon."

I can't believe he took me to Ruth's, the best steakhouse in town. The ambiance and appetizers were the best, and let's not forget the atmosphere.

"Well, what do you think?"

"Well, Ricky, I would say you put your foot in your mouth on this one. Its beautiful."

"Hi, I'm Jesica. Would you two like to order?"

"Um, yes. Let me get your biggest steak with shrimp and garlic sauce and garlic parm noodles. How about you, Lonna?"

"I would like a lobster with salad and garlic bread sticks please."

"And what about drinks?"

"You can give us your most expensive wine for the night. I'm sure you'll pick a good one."

"Yes sir, and would you like any appetizers while you wait?"

"No, thank you."

"Okay, I will be back soon."

"The food is great here."

"Do you remember our first date when we came here, Lonna?"

"Yes, I do. It was the best night of my life."

"Yes, indeed, it was, Lonna. So are you ready for your surprise?"

"Yes, bae, but first let me tell you mine, and then you go. So you know I went to the doctor this morning, and they said I was due for an ultrasound. Well, we are having a boy!"

"What? Lonna, that's great! A boy! I get a boy! That makes me proud."

"Oh, and I have a job up on Capitol Hill, 18 bucks an hour. I can start paying for school."

"Now, wait, Lonna. I'm going to pay for your schooling, and you don't have to work anymore. Be a stay-at-home mom."

"Ricky, I'm not ready for that."

"Baby, it's cool. I got you. I'm going to take care of you. Look, Lonna, will you marry me?"

"What? No, you didn't…"

"Yes, I did."

"Well, the answer to that is a big fat yes!"

"Good, 'cause if yo fucking brother and his goons step to me one more time, I'm going to kill him and beat yo ass fo the bullshit that's coming my way, 'cause yo fat ass can't keep ya damn mouth shut."

"Wait, what are you talking about?"

"You got your brother thinking I'm beating on you, bitch."

"No, that's not true."

"Shut the fuck up fo I slap yo ass all around this room! See, this how it's gonna go—you gonna marry me, have that baby, and act real cool, so your brother can live and yo family, because I will wipe them all out. See, the other day, they rolled up on me talking shit, saying how they gonna bury me fo putting my hands on you, but you know that would be the other way around, so if you love your family, you better be smart about your next move, hoe. Let's go."

Damn, why'd Frank have to go and do that? What the fuck am I gonna do? Damn, I got to call him—damn Frank!

* * *

"Lonna, get the fuck in here now."

"I'm coming."

"Get in here!"

"Yes, Ricky."

"Bend over, let me fuck you."

"I'm not in the mood, Ricky."

"The hell you ain't. Bend the fuck over, or I will take that shit."

The only thing I could feel was the sting from him slapping me in the face.

"Why the fuck do you need to hit me, Ricky?"

"Payback's a bitch, ain't it? Now, bend over."

Oh my God, this is not right…

"Oh Ricky, oh, oh, deeper…"

"Yea, bitch. I know you love when I pump this pussy with hot iron. Yo shit so tight, so wet, just the way I like it. Manm I don't want no other woman but you. Come on, let me lick some pussy."

Why am I allowing this?

"Ohhhh, Ricky… It feels so good. Please don't stop. I want to cum in your mouth."

"Yea, give it all to me, baby, you know you want to."

"Ohhh, ohhh, mmm…Ricky, I'm coming, I'm coming."

"Beg me to fuck you."

"Please, fuck me, Ricky. Please, daddy."

"Louder, I can't hear you!"

"Please, daddy, fuck me and don't stop!"

"Yea, bitch, you mine. I own this shit. Now, suck this dick. Yea, I put that ass to sleep straight up like that. I will see you later."

"Okay, Ricky, have a good day. I love you; your lunch is on the table. I made your favorite."

"Thanks, and don't you leave this house today."

Control. It's all mind control—fuck that, not me.

"Anjala, why did Frank take some boys from the west and pull up on Ricky the other day?"

"What did he do? Oh no… What's wrong with him?"

"I don't know, but I'm in trouble."

"I'm about to call Eric."

Oh hell no.

"Wait, I haven't even talked to Frank yet, and what do you think Eric gonna do, girl? Help us out? Anjala, no, you don't understand. He made me have sex with him and made me beg. He is crazy. I have to play it cool for a while. He said he will kill the whole family. Look, the job called me back and I want to take it, but Ricky has to think I'm still at the diner and told me to stop working and said I had to marry him in order for Frank to stay alive."

"Oh my God, Lonna, we have to end this now. What are you going to do?"

"I don't know yet. I need to talk to Frank. Stay on the line … Hello Frank, what the fuck is wrong with you?"

"I don't know what you're talking about, Lonna."

"Ricky said you and ya goons pulled up on him the other day."

"Yeah, sis, we did, only because we was just riding and spotted him wit this bitch Stacy, who is a chick from the west, and well, sis, I lost it, man. I'm like, man he should be at work, and than I thought about yo face when we was at Mom's party, so I said I owe him one."

"Well, now, he's talking about killing the whole family, Frank, if you don't stay away!"

"What! See what I'm saying, sis? He got to go."

"Frank!"

"No. Nah, sis, I'm going to kill him, and kill him real soon; bury his ass in the dirt."

"What about my son, Frank?"

"I will take care of him, sis, don't worry about that shit. You don't need him, fuck that nigga."

"I'm scared, Frank."

"Sis, I got this. Let me handle it."

"Frank, be careful. And don't get us killed. Frank, please, promise me you're going to come back."

"Sis, I promise I'm coming back. I got to go, Lonna. Hit me later."

CHAPTER 8

"Hey Ricky, I will be back. I'm going out to dinner with my sister and will be back by 10:00."

"Go ahead and remember, don't be stupid, bitch."

"Okay, bae. Love you."

"Hey Tamera, are you ready?"

"Yea, I just picked up Monay and Lex. Is Anjala coming?"

"Yea, she said she will meet us there. Eric will be bringing her."

"Oh shit she got her a new boo, huhj? I hope he's Mr. Right this time."

"Fall back, Tamera, we are still young."

"Whatever, girl. See you soon."

* * *

"Ribs it is! Let's chow down, ladies. So Lex, what's new for you?"

"Well, me and Randy would like to start trying for a baby."

"Oh, that's wonderful, Lex. We are all happy to hear that."

"Thanks, but I'm so excited and exhausted from trying."

"That's funny, Lex."

"Stop it, Tamera. I'm trying my best! So what about you, Tamera, what's new since you're always so damn good?"

"Well, I'm still single and not ready for the drama, if you know what I mean."

"Girl. You better get you a man. Lil' Tim needs a father."

"It's too much for me right now. I can't."

"It's okay, girl. Me and James have our problems, but it's something you work on. If possible, maybe you and big Tim can work on y'all's problems one day."

"Thanks, Lex."

"Oh, guess what, guys!" Monay interjected. "I'm having identical twin girls."

"You about to have another me and Anjala!"

"Oh, hell, you two were trouble! Remember when you snuck out the window, so the two of you could go kiss boys by the lake?"

"Shut up, Tamera."

"So what about you, Anjala?"

"Well, his name is Eric, and I'm happy. I even stopped working at the club. We are also about to move in with each other up on Capitol Hill."

"Wait, what?"

"Yes."

"Anjala—"

"He's a banker."

"Oh gosh!"

"Shut up, Lonna, I know what you told me, but I believe we are going places together."

"Speaking of that, Lonna, I see your new ride outside. Did Ricky get you that?"

"No, Tamera. Anjala brought it for me."

"And what did Ricky have to say about that, haha."

"You know what? Fuck Ricky."

"Well, excuse me, sis. I meant no harm."

"Tamera, you just don't shut up, do you? No wonder you're alone. You're nothing but a shit talker."

"Lonna."

"I'm sorry, Monay. It's just that he's talking about killing us 'cause Frank caught him with another woman from the westside, an' the fact my face was swollen at Mom's birthday party. He told Ricky he was gonna kill him if he ever put his hands on me again."

"Shut up, no way. What you gonna do, Lonna?"

"Fuck that question. Lonna, go to the cops and leave his ass."

"No, it's not that easy, Lex. I don't want anything to happen to you or my son."

"Your son?"

"Yes, it's a boy, Monay."

"Lonna, we are about the same stage of are pregnancy."

"Look, Lonna. We are happy for you, but something needs to be done about Ricky before it goes too far."

"Well, Frank said he's going to handle it."

"Frank does not know what he's doing," Lex said. "He's not even street enough."

"I said I would get Eric to help because he's street smart," Anjala offered.

"Wait, how you got a banker who's street smart?"

"'Cause, Tamera, he is. Now leave it at that."

"Whatever. Anyway, he's got to go. Let's get a hitman to take him out."

"Hell no!" I said. "Look, we gotta keep our mouths shut and let Frank handle it, and don't talk to no one about this. We have are families to think about."

"Well, lil' sis, if you say so," Monay began, "but don't get us all killed. So y'all heard Lonna: Keep your mouths shut. Move as we have been doing. Don't act any different. Oh, I can kill Frank for this shit! Let's all go home."

"Lonna, you sure you don't want to come to my house?" Lex asked.

"I'm sure. I'm going to go home. Call Frank and check on him, but don't let him know you know about this."

Going home, I was not able to sleep. Dream after dream, I wondered what was next. Was he going to kill me while I slept? Shoot me or stab me? I didn't know, but I did not like the feeling I had, and before I woke up, the last dream was an eye opener on just how much I was fed up with Ricky…

* * *

I walked slowly into the room where he laid sound asleep. I saw my shadow every time I passed the room with a little light glaring through. The heavy metal I was holding in my hand was already loaded with one in the chamber, cocked, and ready to put as many in him as it took. I pulled the sheets back and let him know not to make a move because it would be his last. Taking a step back, I aimed for the head—one shot, one kill, execution style, as I was hoping for. Then I let one go, piercing his ear, then another piercing his shoulder, blood flying all over the place. The sight of blood made me want to shoot more, so I let another one go, and this time, it hit his heart. Grabbing his heart and calling my name was the last movement and word he uttered.

* * *

When I awakened, I was pouring sweat and crying. I could not believe I had the balls to kill Ricky, and so it was set. He had to die.

Drinking my coffee and still thinking about that dream I had, I wondered: Could I really do it? Am I tough enough to do this? I don't want to go back to jail. It's no place for a woman who's pregnant anyway. So I picked up the phone to call Frank.

"Hey Frank, I wanted to check on you."

"I'm good, lil' sis. It's going down soon, so stay cool. I got to go."

* * *

Frank

"Yo Ronnie call up the boys. Y'all meet me at the lounge on Westpark Way in about an hour.

Okay, fellas, now you know we rolled up on Ricky the other day. Now he is talking about killing my whole family if Lonna doesn't play it cool."

"I say we roll up on him and put some hot lead in his bitch ass," Ronnie declared.

"Chill, homie, that's what we are here to talk about," Frank replied. "Now y'all know we got to play it cool and do things right. We don't want shit coming back on us. Y'all in or out, Ronnie, Rell, Jay?"

"We are all in, Frank."

"I want it clean and simple. One blow to the back of the head, gravesite needs to be ready ahead of time. Tomorrow, everything goes down. We already know his location."

"Frank, how we gone lower him in or sneak up on him?" Rell asked.

"You know he is always up on Capitol Hill with that one hoe everyday around the same time. He is on drugs, so you know his movement is a lil' slow now. He will be on Main Street, and go old school, just so you all know. Also, the best way is to let him already be high. He not gonna notice the difference of who is serving him, so go that route with him."

"We got ya, Frank."

"Look, don't fuck this up, or all y'all gonna have to go down. My family's life depend on this shit."

"Look, Frank, we got ya," Jay said.

* * *

Lonna

Getting that phone call was like music to my ears, hearing that Mr. Rogers believes that I have a pretty good application was great to know. My thoughts were going 90 miles per hour again—hell, now that I made it to Capitol Hill, there was no way Mom and Dad wouldn't take any money from me now. I couldn't wait; this was what I'd been waiting for. I was really happy for myself. I just couldn't let Ricky find out—he would kill me.

I wondered what Frank was up to. I didn't really want Ricky to die. He was the father of my son. Besides, even with all that was going on, I still had feelings for him and still had a child that needed to know who he was. Life is so unfair at times. Why me, Lord? Why me?

"…I don't know, Anjala. Besides that, I feel like I should have never said anything…"

"No, sis, you did the right thing by telling us all. I mean, who don't want to know if harm or death is standing within 10 feet of us hours on end, ya know? And what about you and the baby? Do you not care what happens to the two of you?"

"Yes, I do care, Anjala. I'm just torn, that's all."

"Okay then, girl, just let Frank handle it. He's not stupid and never road the short bus. I mean, he is not street smart, but he does have connections."

"Did you tell Eric?"

"No, I did not. You asked me not to, so I didn't. But I'm starting to see what you were saying about him not being a banker."

"What do you mean? What happened?"

"Well, he is always out and always on the phone saying he's conversing with other bankers or new customers. I can never bring him lunch. He's telling me I'm a distraction for him."

"Okay, look, Anjala. Don't get mad, but I think he sells drugs."

"Wow, Lonna, that's deep."

"Anjala, I'm just saying."

"No, Lonna, you're going too far with things that you don't even know."

"I apologize for that, Anjala. It's not my place nor my business about what he does. Forgive me for that. As long as he treats you good, it doesn't matter."

"Thanks, Lonna. When I find out, you will be the first to know."

"So you know I'm going to be around a whole bunch of white people with this job."

"So what? You are probably the most educated one there. Stop all the worrying that you're doing. Just because you did not go to college does not make you stupid. You finished all 12 steps without being held back or flunking, something a lot of people can't even do. Look, if he did not like what he read, he would have not called you back. You got this and need this. Shit, I wish I was with you, but no worries, I will stop smoking. Give me about two months, and I will follow."

"It's always good to have you in my corner, Anjala. I just hate admitting when you're right."

"Thanks, girl. Ninety percent of the time I am. Hell, I'm smarter than you think."

"Haha, you know you are."

"Anyway, are you hungry? I want to eat."

"Sure. But only if you're making that famous clam chowder and fried chicken though."

"No way, love. You have to place an order for that two days in advance."

"Let me take this call, it's Frank … Hey Frank, everything okay?"

"Look Lonna, just listen. It's going down tomorrow."

"No, Frank, this can't happen. Let me just put him in jail."

"Look, sis, it is what it is."

"Frank, Frank. Frank!"

"Damn, girl. What's the problem?"

"Frank said he killing Ricky tomorrow!"

"Do you really think he has the heart to do it?"

"No, Anjala. He doesn't. But his friends do. I don't believe he's going to kill him, just shake him up a bit and put him in his place."

"Well, I hope so, 'cause I see you have had a change of heart, Ms. Lonna. Look, Lonna, I'm not sure what's about to happen, but you can't wreck your brain about this. Ricky gonna wind up killing you and the baby. He stays drunk all the time; he might black out and hurt you.

And you don't want that to happen. Shit, if I was you I would have left him with the first hit he laid upon my ass. You know you can be a silly woman at times, and it's time for you to grow up and be a real woman, a grown woman. Know what you want and let your concerns be about that baby, Lonna, not a man who beats on you. You're beautiful."

"Okay, Anjala. I'm going to this interview and will try an' let things go. I'm just going to break things off with Ricky tonight and move forward with my life. I'm about to go home."

"Wait, I thought you were going to stay and eat?"

"I'm no longer hungry. I will just lay down until Ricky gets home and spray the bad news."

"Girl, you done gassed me up and shit, but I understand. Go get you some rest. Please be careful. You know what he told you if you were to leave him."

"Anjala, I know. He might just be too drunk to believe me. I will pack a bag and come back here."

CHAPTER 9

"Lonna, Lonna. Wake up. Did you cook? I'm hungry."

"Food is in the oven."

"Come on, warm it up for me."

"Okay, 'cause I would like to talk to you anyway. Look, Ricky, I really do love you unconditionally, and we have come a long way. All the fighting that's going on is not good for us or the baby. I'm stressed out and can't focus on things, and I really don't believe you will kill us over some stupid stuff. I'm hoping we can just go talk things over with my brother and show him it's not what he thinks."

"No, Lonna. See, it doesn't work like that, you dumb bitch. See, I'm a man, and he's a man. We got pride an' ain't no talking. He wants problems, he has them. And as for you, well, you better hope I let you live after this is all over."

"Ricky, are you serious? Look, it's just time we separate. I can't and will no longer deal with this from you. My life is full of shit. I owe my family money, and you're not helping me pay any of it back. You drank up all my money for college, and I have lied to my family countless of times to pay our bills. This is absurd. I am just tired of trying with no change as the outcome. I can't believe you have allowed yourself to become this worthless liar who stands in front of me to feed me shit off the floor and tell me I have no choice but to deal with it. It stops today. You are going to leave, or

I will. I'm not scared of you, Ricky. I'm not scared, and you're cheating on me. I'm not letting you get away with this shit, sitting around waiting on you hand and foot, waiting for the next blow to my face, waiting to know the moment I have to be rushed to the ER because you hurt me that bad—or worse, killed my unborn child."

All I could feel was my face stinging, bones shattering, and blurred vision. I heard him saying, "Shut the fuck up, Lonna. You belong to me, therefore abide by my rules. There's no way around it, babe. Just suck it up and deal with it. Maybe one day you will be able to meet her, and we can all be one big happy family. I can't even believe you're pregnant. Hell, is it mine? You probably fucked a nigga at the diner. I'm gone for the night, and when I return, you better be here, or we gonna have problems that need to be solved."

Calling Anjala was the last thing I wanted to do, but I had to.

"Hello? Lonna, are you okay? Lonna, can you hear me?"

"Yes, I'm on my way over."

'Did he hit you? Hello? Hello? Lonna, talk to me, baby girl."

"You're right, Anjala. There's no telling what's going to happen, but you know what? I hope Frank does kill him. He needs to die. He slapped me around so much, and the blows were so powerful, I have broken bones in my face and blurred vision in one eye. He told me I belong to him. On top of all that, it hurts 'cause I'm always trying to fix our problems and make it work because I still loved him."

"Okay, look. Lonna, let's go to the ER and get your face checked out. You have a big day tomorrow and need some rest. 'Cause you know what? Love hurts, life hurts. There's no such existence of the two without pain or sorrow, baby girl. You just have to learn how to hurdle through it."

* * *

"I'm going to go to bed. Eric is here."

"Come here, babe, and give me your body. You have been gone all day and have some making up to do. Damn, boo, you stay on your knees all night like that, and I'm telling you, I have no problem with that, but you keep sucking this dick like that, and I will have nothing left to penetrate you with. I do want some pussy."

"Oh, stop it, Eric. Look, Lonna is in trouble. Ricky fractured some bones in her face. We were at the ER all night. Hold me and tell me you will never do me like that."

* * *

"Lonna, how are you feeling? And good morning. I made you breakfast. Are you hungry? Also you need to be getting up. It's time to get ready."

"I'm doing okay. How did your night go with Eric?"

"Girl, he had me doing a headstand, sucking him off while he ate my pussy. I think I came like 100 times over and over again. Did you sleep well?"

"Yes, I did. Like a baby. I sure did not hear y'all's loud asses."

"Good, I'm glad you got some rest. Eric said he will be gone all day today because he has a big deal with a major company today. While you're gone, I will look for some good movies, and we both can chill and have the girls over for movie night maybe."

"Sounds good. I got to go. Love you."

* * *

"Ms. Lonna Stone! Mr. Rogers will see you now. If you will be as kind to follow me. My name is Lidea. Can I offer you coffee along the way or perhaps some water?"

"Water would be great, if you don't mind."

"No, not at all, honey. See we are on the first floor, and we have to make our way to the twelfth floor, so you see, I don't mind. And I have to pick Mr. Rogers up a cup of coffee. We have a very large company, and he wants to expand the building, too. Well, not that he needs to with 12 floors an' all, but hey, who am I to say what doesn't need to be done? If I may ask, what position did you apply for?"

"I applied for tech support for the in- and out-bound calls." Gosh this lady talks way too much…

"I don't know, honey. Mr. Rogers has been talking about your interview all morning. You sure that's what you applied for? Anyway, here we are."

"Come in, come in!"

"Here you are, Mr. Rogers. Your 9:00 a.m. appointment with Ms. Stone, and your cup of coffee with two message returns.

And your wife said don't forget dinner is at 8:00. Be there, or be square."

"Thank you, Lidea. You may leave us now. Hello Ms. Stone. As you know, I'm Mr. Rogers. Glad you could make it, and on time may I say. You know being on time is the key to success."

"Thank you, Mr. Rogers. I'm glad to meet you."

"Okay, Lonna. Take a seat. I see you applied for tech support. Do you believe you qualify for this position?"

"Why, yes, Mr. Rogers. I do."

"But Ms. Stone, you don't. I know you are overqualified for the position. As a matter of fact, I would like to offer you to be my personal assistant. Would that be something you're interested in?"

"Oh, wow, Mr. Rogers, are you sure? I mean, yes. That would be great."

"Good, Lonna. That means your pay rate will change down to $10 an hour."

"What!"

"No, no, Lonna. I'm just kidding. That will put you at $23 an hour. Your pay rate will go up to $30 an hour after one year, with holiday bonuses. Also, you will handle daily tasks such as making daily runs, getting coffee, picking up cases, finding ways to beat cases, taking phone calls and messages, and last but not least, attending meetings with me. You're my sidekick Lonna, is that okay with you?"

"Yes sir."

"Good. You will be from at 9:00 a.m. to 5:00 p.m., or as needed for overtime. If you do have to work overtime, you will get paid your $23, plus night shift bonus. Are we clear, Ms. Stone?"

"Yes sir."

"And one more thing, Ms. Stone. I expect to see you at holiday parties and events. No exceptions, Ms. Stone. You may start tomorrow if you like. No—how about Monday, so you can have a fresh start without rushing. A week is more than enough time to prioritize your personal life, and you can get the swing of things."

"Got you. Monday 9:00 a.m sharp, I will be here. Thank you again, Mr. Rogers."

"No problem, Lonna. Welcome to Capitol Hill! Have a great day."

* * *

"Oh my gosh! I just want to scream… I finally made it! All my dreams have come true, and I don't know where to start!"

"Good, sis! You deserve it! Plus, you're a smart woman. Now you can pay me my thousand I lent you back freely with no worries, ya know?"

"Ugh! I know! Don't remind me. By the way, have you heard from Ricky?"

"No. Should I have?"

"No, just asking. We got into a fight yesterday, and he left. I haven't heard from him since. You know he always calls you if he returns home and I'm not there, that's all."

"No, sis. He has not called me or come over, okay? Give it to about noon. He should be back by then. I love you, sis, will call you later."

"Oh, wait, Monay, do you want to have a movie night with the girls? If so, call me and come on over to Anjala's."

* * *

"Hello ladies. Thanks for coming. I ordered pizza, chicken, subs, and got soda, tea, and water. Is everyone okay with that?"

"Yes, we are!"

"Well, damn, Anjala. You and Eric have a very nice house. It's really nice, ya know? It's really big! You guys must have spent a fortune on this bad babe."

"Thanks, Lex, but I'm not sure Eric paid for all of this."

"And you're not concerned how he got all this nice, big ol' house? You don't worry that you left everything you worked for behind?"

"You know, Monay, I'm the last person you need to worry about. And just to keep you updated, I always have a backup plan, but now is not the time to question me about my life. Anyway, how is yours?"

"Hm, no complaints, honey."

"Okay, y'all! Let's stop this. Monay, you are always nitpicking. You need to chill."

"Thanks, Tamera."

"You're welcome. So Lonna, what movies do we have? And Anjala, is Eric here?"

"No, he's going to be out for the night."

"We have Dead Man Walking, When the Sky Falls, Darkness Upon Us, Who's Yo Mama, and Don't Look Twice."

"Oh, gosh. You guys suck at movie hunting! Let's go with Who's Yo Mama, something funny first."

"Shut up, Tamera. I tried."

CHAPTER 10

Let's Continue

"Question: Has anyone heard from June?"

"I have. He's out of town. He said he will be gone for a few weeks."

"Good looking, Lex, but why won't he pick up his phone is the question."

"Lonna, you know he doesn't want to be bothered when he's away. Hell, if you ask me, he be with a woman."

"Oh, no, Lex! Don't say that!"

"Shit, I rather it be that. I thought my brother was gay."

"Shut up, Tamera. You can never think that you're silly for that."

"Okay, okay, Lonna. Come on, y'all, movie time."

* * *

Frank

"Shit, Frank. It's Ronnie. We all here, man. I see this nigga now; he look fucked up. Rell sold him some shit without much cut on it, so he feeling real good right now."

"What's his location?"

"He talking to lil' shorty from the west right now, the same place we rolled up on him at."

"That must be the lil' bitch honeycomb hideout. Look, watch him closely, and when you see him not being able to hold his composure anymore, go in for the kill. Remember, one shot to the back of the head, hands and feet bound, grave dug, and gun wiped clean, broken down, and tossed in different parts of the river. Burner phone chips out and burned clothing. Also, leave no DNA. Burn the car in the next town; come collect the money."

"Got ya, man. Will hit you once it's done."

"Frank, call me. It's Lonna. Call me back. Don't do anything stupid. I'm with the girls."

"Shit, Lonna, what the hell you want?"

You have reached the voicemail box of Chicago leave a message after the beep.

"Frank, it's Ronnie. I need you to call me back ASAP."

"Look, Lonna, now is not the time. I will call you later … Ronnie, what's the news?"

"Frank, it's all bad, Frank."

"What the fuck you talking about? Please explain and do so slowly."

"Some cats just pulled up on Ricky, put a bag over his head, shot ol' girl in the face and took Ricky with them."

"What? Nigga, you playing."

"Nah, man. That's what happened. What you want us to do?"

"You know what? Slide out. Our hands are clean. Whoever took his ass 'bout to do it for us. Be cool. I will hit you up later. Don't say shit to no one."

* * *

Lonna

"Thank you ladies for coming over. I had fun. We should do this more often."

"Lonna, are you staying or going home?"

"I will go home to see if Ricky made it back. I don't know, Anjala. I have a bad feeling."

"Girl, I don't know why you give a fuck about that nigga! I mean, why do you care the way you do?"

"Anjala, not right now, okay?"

"Sorry, boo. Call me let me know what's going on."

* * *

"No, he's not home, so I'm going to soak in a bubble bath and call Mike."

"What? Girl, you got his number?"

"Yes, girl. I thought I told you. Anyway, I'm going to call him. Goodnight, Anjala."

"Hello?"

"Hi, it's Lonna."

"I was wondering when you would call, my queen. I saw you at the market the other day, and you did not look my way, as always."

"It's not that. I'm just going through some things, ya know? And now I'm trying to free myself."

"Well, my queen, you have called the right person for that. What are you doing as we speak?"

"Taking a bubble bath."

"Is the water hot enough for you, my queen?"

"Yes, it is."

"Would you like me to come over and help you out?"

"No—I mean, I don't know when Ricky will come back."

"Well, you can come over to my place."

"No. I prefer conversation with you over the phone for now, like picking your brain, knowing who you are from child to adult, your favorite color and then some."

"As do I, my queen. No rush. Just wanted to help ease your mind and see your beautiful face."

"Thank you, Mike. Most appreciated. So tell me about yourself, Mike."

"How about you first, Lonna."

"Okay, well, I'm 22 going on 23, five months pregnant, and just landed a job up on Capitol Hill. I have my high school crush who I've been with giving me the blues, and I want to just leave it all be-hind and move forward and pay my loving family back all their money I owe them. See, they put up a whole lot of money for me for collage, and I spent it all up on my boyfriend, bills, and myself and never went to college. The whole time they thought I was in college, I was living with him, wasting my life and getting controlled and beat every step of the way."

"Damn, my queen, you was that starstruck over this man? I see. But it be like that when it's your first rodeo with a man or woman, I can dig that. You're pregnant? What you having?"

"A boy."

"Is this your first one?"

"Yes."

"Cool, my queen. Congratulations. So about me. I'm 26 years old, work at the market, been here in Knox all my life. My mom and dad are both deceased. I am an only child. I'm putting money away, so I can partner up with the market and get a few of my own. No wife, no woman. I have my own place not far from Capitol Hill. I would like to get married and have a few babies. Ya know, get that nice little house, grow old, and die happy. I am a straight-forward guy, very articulate, spontaneous, ambitious, strong, and a little on the wild side."

"Wow, Mike. That sounds good!"

"Yes, thank you. And I would like for you to be that lady to lay with me and be happy, Lonna."

"But you don't even know me."

"Just give me a chance, and I know you, my queen. Give me a chance. Let me take you out on a date, my queen. There's a boat ride coming up this weekend, and I would love to take you."

"Okay, but only because you talk so cute. You have a very deep voice. It's magnificent. Maybe your calling is to be a singer! It sounds like Barry White."

"Thank you, my queen. So look, Lonna, you go ahead and relax. It's about 2:00 a.m., and I have to be to work at 7:00. When you see me at the market, don't forget to speak."

"Okay, Mike. Goodnight. Have a beautiful day."

* * *

Ricky

"Man, look, please don't kill me, man. I have a family at home, two kids, and a wife. Look, I got money. I got money, man. Whatever it is that you want I got, you can have it all, just spare me my life, man. Look, just call my wife. Her name's Lonna Stone. She will give you whatever you ask for, man. Just tell her what you want. Just don't kill me."

"Nigga, shut the fuck up. And what you say yo wife's name is?"

"Lonna, man."

"Word that's yo girl; small world. I wonder how she would feel knowing how much of a pathetic punk bitch you really are, sitting here begging for your life, not even knowing or trying to find out who this man is that's about to kill yo punk ass. You a drunk, dope head ass nigga who can't pay his way through shit, depending on berries to feed yo habits and make money for you. Very flawed of you, my nigga. Fucking these nasty ass hoes."

"Wait, you know Lonna?"

"Don't worry about all that, let's get to why you played me and my boys on our last run, Mr. Toughguy. What? You thought we was gonnna let that shit ride?"

"Wait, Lonna put you up to this shit? Or her bitch ass brother."

"What the fuck you talking about, man? Need I remind you, or start by cutting yo damn fingers off?"

"Yo, Bill, start cutting this nigga fingers off, so we can refresh his memory."

"Okay, okay, look, man. I was out of money; thought I had it all together. I was working on it for you."

"Nah, see, how I see it is you were too busy getting lit off your own supply and giving in to them damn berries for the last few weeks. I've been keeping my eye on you. See, you owe me $40,000, and if I let you slide, then other niggas gonna think they can do the same. So you are my first example on how not to fuck with me."

"Flex, man. I got yo money, man; I got ya, money."

"Nah, man. You don't. But talk is cheap. Let's end this. See, I know you did not buy ya girl that nice lil' car she got. Also, I know the place of employment of that pretty lil' chunkie faced bitch of yours. I also know she is not your wife, neither do you have kids, so that means you have nothing to lose here."

"Bill, Jordan! Get in here. Hey, can you believe his bitch is the chick Lonna from the diner? And I just put two and two together: the chick Lonna my girl be talking about, that's her people. Really, just a small world, ha!"

"Hell yea, man. That's crazy."

"Hey Bill, tell Mr. Richy Rich how you gonna fuck his wife every night, make her get down and suck ya dick every night, fuck the brains out of that baby of his she carryin'. Tell him how you gave her 300 bucks after she served you a plate full of pussy fo breakfast at the diner and how much she was begging for that ass to get smacked. But he got 40 G's laying around, and his bitch works at a diner making what $2 an hour. Get real. You see, Ricky, I have yo life in my hands, and Lonna's, 'cause if she ever found out about me killing you, I would have to take her out—and ya lil' man, too."

"No, man. Please, be cool. I will have your money tomorrow, and please don't kill Lonna. I love that woman."

"Hell, I can't tell, my man. You probably done gave that woman HIV sleeping around. Oh, and ya lil' boo, she gone bye, bye. Had my nigga put one in the brain. That shit was gruesome—brains all over the place, her begging to us to spare her life, all while ya dick was still in her hands. Boy, she really had ya."

"Yo, E. Enough. Let me kill this nigga."

"Wait, E. I don't know you; you got the wrong guy."

"Nigga, cause it's Flex to you."

"You 'bout to have a slow, painful death, my nigga," Bill said. "They gonna have to pull dental records on ya…if they ever find you."

"You will not get away with this! And you better hope I don't live, 'cause well, then it will be your turn to suffer."

"I'm done with this fool. Y'all do what y'all do best: kill this nigga … Oh, is this your phone ringing? Hmm, its Lonna. She must really care about you. Don't even see how she put up with you."

* * *

Lonna

"You have reached Ricky you know what to do."

"Ricky, we need to talk. Call me back when you get this message. Let me know if you're coming home or not. Look, Ricky, I love you…"

* * *

Ricky

"I guess she won't be getting a call back, now will she? Kill this fool. Call me when it's done."

CHAPTER 11

Let's Finish This!

Bill

"Man, that fool never stood a chance, J," I said.

"He was weak as fuck, ya know?" Jordan replied.

"I got a better chance of fucking Lonna now. Shit, who she gonna run too once she find out he not coming back?"

"Shit, you know what was funny, Bill man, when you hit that nigga with that crowbar. I promise you, half his teeth came out."

"Yep, screaming like a bitch."

"Man, remind me to stay on ya good side my nigga," Jordan laughed.

"You know you, my nigga, we go way back. I will never turn on you. Just keep in mind, J don't ever fuck me over to make me change my mind. Let's go to the club and have a drink shit celebrate a job well done."

* * *

"Yo, E. It's done. We took that nigga out," I told Eric.

"What y'all do with the body?"

"We left his lifeless-ass body out by Oak Park. Let the animals take a bite out his ass. By time they do find him most of the body will be gone."

"You sure he's dead?" he asked.

"Shit, man, he dead," I assured him. "J cut some fingers and toes off. I stabbed him a few times, hit him with a crowbar, sliced his throat, and shot his ass. If that did not kill him, I don't know what would. No pulse, though. J checked."

"Good, homie. That's what's up. Tell J good looking. What're y'all doing now?"

"Having a celebration on a lil' death victory, something I love doing: racking up bodies. Are you coming to join us?"

"Nah, I'm heading home. Got some shit to do. Will link with y'all tomorrow. Get rid of the phone and clean y'all selves up."

* * *

Anjala

"Hey, babe, how was your day? You know you've been gone all day helping them people. It's 4:00 a.m."

"Nah just needed some time to think. I had some other stuff going on. Let me ask you something, Anjala. So Lonna yo people by blood?"

"Yes, why?"

"'Cause you know before you and me was official, she served me and my boys over at the diner."

"Oh, did she, babe? I told you she was cool."

"Yeah, but look. Let me talk to you about some real shit, Anjala, and I need you to understand 'cause this shit deep right here. You need to know if you down with me."

"Wait—hell no. What did you do to my cousin?"

"Look, yo fam good. I haven't touched her. It's just deep, so hear me out. I'm from Cleveland, and it is very true, but what's not true is being a banker. I came here to make more money. I am a high-time drug dealer. I got the word that Knox high time players here up on Capitol Hill, so i had to give it a try and blow some heat off my ass back in Cleveland."

"Eric, you could have told me this. It's not about what you do, but how you treat me."

"No, Anjala, it's more. Look I was not even supposed to be with you. You were just a chick I had to pull to stay low and have a stash house, but I'm falling in love with you, Anjala."

"I see."

"I thought this was real from the get-go, so did we surpass that part now right?"

"Yes, we did."

"Truth is, I have had a chance to meet powerful people here, and some non-powerful people point out that I met your cousin dude Ricky, and he owes me $40,000. He's been playing me about my money, so I had to bodie him."

"What did you do, kill him?"

"Yeah and that lil' bitch he been fucking wit from the west."

"Oh my God, why are you telling me this?"

"Because Anjala, I love you, and I need you to know who I am, what I'm capable of doing, and how you get a chance to live this life even if it hurts you."

"You know, Lonna told me it was more to you, and I did not believe her."

"What does she know about me?"

"Nothing. She said you was too street to be a banker, that's all."

"Okay, look Anjala, just keep your mouth shut. Don't even be telling Lonna shit."

"Look, Eric, Lonna's brother Frank had a hit out on Ricky, too. They were watching him too. Yesterday was supposed to be the day they took him out."

"What? Are you serious? I wonder if they saw us than. Damn, Anjala. I need to get in contact with them."

"No. No, you don't. This how it needs to be played. If Frank had a hit out on him, right, whenever they find the body—or if the body is ever found, the thought process is already in our heads that Frank and his boys did it. See, Frank don't know who you are. Wait…were you at the scene?"

"Yeah, but I never got out of the car, and we had masks on."

"Okay, good. Then your cover was not blown. Let's play this by ear. Come on, I have something nice for you in the bedroom. Let's relax."

* * *

"Damn, you sure do know how to put a nigga down. That's why I love you. When you gonna have my baby?"

"The sooner you shut up and slide that big dick in me wit yo sexy ass… Oh, oh, oh—shit, Eric, I'm cuming—don't stop! Damn the way you kiss me all over my body makes me melt like butter pecan ice cream on top of a banana split. Keep kissing me… You make me feel all warm inside. I've never had a man like you. I just want to make love to you all day."

"You never had a man love you?"

"No."

"How could I not? You have the body of a goddess and a mouth of pure heaven. You put me in as a trance, woman, and got my feet shaking an' shit, nutting five or more times. Who does that shit?"

"Me. Let's go eat, babe."

"Nah, Anjala, just lay here with me, baby. I just want to hold you. You never know what's gonna happen with the type of life I live."

"Okay, baby."

* * *

Ricky

"What the fuck is going on? Where am I?"

"Don't worry, sir. You are in Knoxville Trauma Center. My name is Ann, and you're in the recovery room. You were found about three weeks ago unconscious and losing a lot of blood. We have been taking care of you. Do you by any chance remember your name, sir?"

"No, I don't… I don't even know what happened to me. Wait what happened to my fingers, my teeth…and why is this stuff on my face?"

"Sir, I am not sure, but you came in with three fingers cut off. We were able to put them back on for you. Your teeth were missing, and your face was disfigured. We put you back together as well as we could. You will have to meet with Doctor Rose and Doctor Navarie. They are your surgical doctors."

"What the fuck is this shit? Get me out of here!"

"I'm sorry, sir. You also suffer from two broken ribs and a punctured lung. You

were knocking on death's door. We have you down as John doe until we find out who you are or family for you."

* * *

Anjala

"I'm telling you, Anjala, he hasn't come home in three weeks. Phone is going to vmail, and now I'm scared something is wrong. Do you think Frank really killed him?"

"Girl, no. He probably just ran off. Shit, ain't no telling, so what I'm telling you is that you need to chill and worry about you. The baby is due soon, and you and Mike are doing good. Just keep moving forward. Live a little."

"But his family has been calling me, what do I tell them?"

"Nothing, because you honestly don't know where he is. Tell them he's been strung out on drugs and drinking heavily, and you believe he left you for another woman…"

"Wait, Anjala, this shit crazy. I'm about to turn the TV up. Listen to this…"

"Breaking News. I am Stoney Brooks, and I am here live with you today in a location near Capitol Hill on West Street where a body of a unidentified woman was recovered, believed to be white or of Hispanic descent. If anyone can help identify her, call crisis help line. She has a tattoo with the name of Ricky on her right arm…"

"Anjala, did you hear that? I'm calling the cops!"

"Lonna, just leave it alone. Stay away from this shit!"

"Really, Anjala, I can't."

"Yes the fuck you can, and you will! I'm tired of you doing this to yourself about a rude, self-centered bastard of man!"

"Okay, Anjala, okay, but what if he's still alive or dead?"

Damn Lonna, I wish i could tell you he's dead, so you could feel better and move on with your life.

* * *

Lonna

It's been two months now and not a word from him. Part of me is happy about it, and part of me is not whole. I don't know I feel, as if I'm breaking down and need to find a way to rebuild myself.

As I'm going over this to myself in my head my phone rings.

"Hello, this is Makalla, a nurse over at the University of Tennessee Medical Center. I have a John Doe here, and we are calling contacts in his phone to find out who he is. Your number is on the list to call. Do you have a family member missing?"

"I'm sorry, Makalla. No, I don't. Sorry I can't help you."

To be continued...

www.ingramcontent.com/pod-product-compliance
Lightning Source LLC
Chambersburg PA
CBHW071457030726
47593CB00003B/1040